GHOST RIDERS
PLANES, TRAINS & AUTOMOBILES

BARBARA SMITH

GHOST
HOUSE

Ghost House Books

The Publisher: Ghost House Books
Distributed by Lone Pine Publishing
10145 – 81 Avenue
Edmonton, AB T6E 1W9
Canada

1808 – B Street NW, Suite 140
Auburn, WA 98001
USA

Website: http://www.ghostbooks.net

Library and Archives Canada Cataloguing in Publication

Smith, Barbara, 1947—
    Ghost riders : planes, trains and automobiles / Barbara Smith.

    Includes bibliographical references.
    ISBN 1-894877-56-X
    1. Ghosts—Juvenile literature. I. Title.

GR580.S63 2004   J398.25   C2004-903437-5

Editorial Director: Nancy Foulds
Project Editor: Chris Wangler
Production Manager: Gene Longson
Layout and Production: Chia-Jung Chang
Book Design: Curtis Pillipow
Cover Design: Elliot Engley

Illustrations: Aaron Norell

The stories, folklore and legends in this book are based on the author's research of sources including individuals whose experiences have led them to believe they have encountered phenomena of some kind or another. They are meant to entertain, and neither the publisher nor the author claims these stories represent fact.

We acknowledge the financial support of the Government of Canada through the Book Publishing Industry Development Program (BPIDP) for our publishing activities.

PC: 06

For Sam, Luke, Kyle and Kate
May you always be in good spirits!

TABLE OF CONTENTS

NOTE FROM THE AUTHOR

Ghosts are everywhere, it seems. Over the years I've spent collecting true ghost stories, I've realized that the more you investigate the world of the paranormal, the more ghost stories you find. Even so, I was surprised when I started find ghost stories involving vehicles! How could an object that was never alive become a ghost? And how could phantom ships be among the world's oldest supernatural tales?

And then there are stories about phantoms haunting cars and trains, and even roads and bridges. As you read the stories in this book, you may begin to wonder, as I do, if the ghostly combinations might be endless. While you're wondering, keep in mind that all these stories were inspired by actual events. Real people just like you and me have experienced the encounters re-told here!

Now, lock the car in the garage, turn down the lights and read all about haunted planes, trains, automobiles and more!

Hauntingly yours,
Barbara Smith

LANDING
A MIRACLE

From the time Bobbie George was just a few weeks old, his father had taken him for airplane rides. By 1966, when the child was four years old, Fletcher George and his son were still enjoying flying over the mountains of Kenya, Africa.

In the early evening of October 19, the two boarded Fletcher's small Cessna airplane. The planned trip was not unusual, because Fletcher George was the pilot for a mining company and he was needed in another part of Kenya. There was no reason to suspect that this flight would be anything but just another ordinary journey for father and son.

Both Bobbie and Fletcher were always silent as the older man taxied the plane down the runway and lifted it into the air. After that, even when Bobbie was far too young to understand a word his father said to him, Fletcher would talk to his son and explain everything he was doing to fly the small plane.

That is how this flight in October began.

Once the small plane was off the ground and Fletcher had reached the right altitude, the man turned to his son, who sat quietly in the seat beside him.

"Want to come and sit here with me?" he asked little Bobbie, who answered by clambering across to his father's lap. There the two of them sat, staring first out the cockpit window, and then at the array of dials on the instrument panels in front of them.

Bobbie eventually crawled back into his own seat. Everything was going well—until Fletcher felt a terrible crushing pain in his chest.

Frightened that he might lose consciousness, the man reached for the radio to contact the nearest airport. He needed to let people on the ground know that he was sick and could not keep flying. He had to land the plane right away.

But Fletcher's hand never even made it as far as the radio's handset. His chest pain was caused by a massive heart attack. Fletcher George was dead, and four-year-old Bobbie was left alone in a plane drifting dangerously low over mountains. It seemed inevitable that the plane would crash.

Some minutes after Fletcher's body slumped to the side of the pilot's seat, the staff at an isolated Kenyan airstrip saw a strange sight just over the horizon. It looked as though a plane was preparing to land on their runway! The workers knew that they weren't expecting any aircraft that day, and so this landing was probably an emergency. As quickly as they could, they prepared for the possibility of a crash. Once those preparations were made, they huddled together in the tower to watch the plane.

Much to their surprise, the approaching plane flew between two mountain peaks before gently descending onto the waiting ribbon of tarmac. With the exception of a few wobbles, the plane touched down for a perfect three-point landing and then slowly rolled to a stop.

The workers in the tower all raced toward the aircraft to congratulate the pilot on an excellent landing on such a difficult airstrip. The first man to reach the plane unlatched and opened its door. Then he froze in complete disbelief. There, before him, was a child, a little boy who could not even have been old enough to go to school. The child was

sitting on the seat beside a dead body slumped to the side.

"My dad got sick," little Bobbie told the man as he was lifted down from the cockpit.

"But who landed the plane?" the man asked.

"I did, I guess," Bobbie replied. "My dad always told me what to do and I just remembered and did those things, so I'm here."

None of those gathered around said a word. They all knew that they'd just witnessed an extraordinary event—far more extraordinary than a child flying an airplane through mountainous terrain and then safely landing it on a little-known airstrip. They had just witnessed a father's devotion outliving his physical body. For no matter how much a four-year-old knew about flying, he was simply not tall enough to reach the rudder pedals or the handle to set the flaps.

No, that plane had been landed by someone or something from far, far beyond the skies as we flesh-and-blood human beings know them. The spirit of Bobbie's father landed that plane—while his body lay lifeless on the pilot's seat.

SINKING SPIRITS

A long time ago, a ship left its home harbor of Chicago, Illinois, heading through the Great Lakes to Buffalo, New York. Shortly after the voyage began, a sharp-eyed sailor noticed something wrong with one of the sails way up at the highest point of the ship's topmost mast. The man ran to explain the problem to the captain, who ordered two of the crew's youngest sailors to climb the ship's rigging until they reached that highest point and fixed what was broken. No one knows exactly what happened next, but seconds after the young men reached the top of the mast, they fell to the deck. Both sailors died instantly.

The dead men's co-workers were shocked and saddened by the accident. They were also terrified. Sailors are very superstitious, and one of the worst omens is for a death to occur aboard a ship. Two deaths as a result of just one accident was simply too much for these seafarers to bear. Every man on board wanted to get off the ship immediately, but the captain was greedy and thought only of the money he would make if he delivered the cargo to its destination. He refused to turn the ship around and sail back to their home port. The frightened sailors had no choice but to try to make it through to Buffalo.

By evening, the weather had turned cold, and frigid lake spray washed up on the deck of the ship. These dangerous conditions, and knowing that two corpses lay in the ship's hold, were too much for the sailors. They pleaded with the captain to turn the craft around, but he wouldn't hear of it.

The stubborn captain knew he had to do something for his men because it was never a good idea to sail with an unhappy crew. In an attempt to distract them, the man offered the sailors as much food as they wanted throughout the voyage instead of their usual daily rations. Because it was nearly dinnertime when he made his announcement, the sailors hungrily agreed to accept their boss' offer. Soon the men were all back working at their posts.

That evening, before slinging up their hammocks for the night, the ship's crew held a prayer service for the men who had died. A proper funeral would have to wait until they were on shore again, but for now they could at least show their respects for their former mates. "Rest in peace," they wished the deceased.

Sadly, that wish would not be granted. The ship's crew was about to find out that the souls of the recently deceased were very restless.

As midnight approached, the sailors' hammocks squeaked and moaned under their sleeping bodies. It wasn't the sound of the ship's timbers creaking as the small craft was tossed about on the dark waves that disturbed the men. Those were noises that experienced sailors were used to hearing, and so they slept on. It was the eerie sounds of ghostly wails and cries and sighs echoing from the hold that woke up the men. If a sailor had been sleeping deeply enough to miss the sad, unnatural sounds, the terrified screams of his mates would certainly have wakened him.

Moments later, long, dark, shadows in the form of two human beings could be seen floating about the room. The frigid air turned even icier wherever these evil-looking shadows appeared. As the dark forms hovered above the sailors' hammocks, the men could see cold, glistening eyes staring down at them. The sight confirmed that the seafaring superstition was accurate. A death during a voyage *was* an evil sign. Their ship was haunted.

The men brave enough to move scrambled out of their hammocks and up the ladder onto the deck. They huddled together in terror until the sun came up. As soon as the captain awoke, the sailors told him that the ship must sail for a safe port as fast as possible. There were two on board, they explained, who were no longer human.

Realizing that there was no way to calm his crew, the captain ordered the men to sail the haunted ship to Buffalo as fast as it could go. In record time, the vessel docked. Instead of waiting to claim their wages, the sailors fled from the cursed ship. The captain himself had to carry the dead bodies ashore, hoping his problems had ended.

They hadn't.

Even with the bodies gone, his crew refused to return to the ship. It was jinxed forever, they told the captain. Worse, the sailors spread word of the haunting to every sailor in town. Not one man would sign on for the ship's trip back to Chicago. The captain and his unlucky ship were stranded in Buffalo.

The troubled ship remained docked for days and then weeks and finally months—abandoned. Well, almost abandoned. Anyone unfortunate enough to be on the dock beside it at night knew that the ship was actually full of life. Afterlife, that is. Some nights, it was positively alive with ghostly activity.

Dozens of dock workers reported horrible, inhuman cries coming from the deserted ship's hold. Strange balls of light were seen dancing about the highest point of the now-rotting mast. These horrors continued for years and years while the haunted ship remained where it had been docked.

Finally, when its timbers had thoroughly rotted, the ship began to sink. Not even one piece of wood was salvaged from it. Everyone in the sailing community knew it was best to simply let nature take her course with the haunted ship.

As far as anyone knows, the ghosts of the dead sailors went down with their ship. Since the haunted old tub finally sank, there have been no phantom lights or ghostly cries anywhere near the dock.

And so it seems that at least one old seafaring superstition is more than just a legend. In this case, death aboard a ship most certainly did bring terror.

RIDING WITH WRAITHS

On the first Tuesday afternoon in September, Jeff was about as happy as a kid could be. He'd spent the summer at his grandparents' farm, and although he'd enjoyed his holiday, he was very glad to be back home with his family in the city.

For Jeff, the best part about being at the farm had been all the hard physical work he'd done. He was way stronger now than he had been last spring, and he figured he'd have no trouble making his school's baseball team this year.

Right now, though, all he had to do was catch the bus home from his first day back at school. He smiled at that thought because this year was the first year he didn't have to ride on a school bus. Those stuffy, bumpy bus rides with kids acting like idiots had been fun when he was younger, but for the past couple of years, Jeff had truly hated the trips. Now, finally, he was old enough to take public transit.

Leaning up against the bus shelter Jeff thought he saw the bus coming. He picked up his backpack and took out his bus pass. When the bus was a block away, the boy moved closer to the curb.

Jeff squinted into the sunshine. *The afternoon light's sure funny in the fall,* he thought. *That bus looks like it's painted green. Weird. City buses are red and white.* Little did Jeff know then that bus colors were about to become very important in his life.

Seconds later, an ugly old green bus pulled over to the curb in front of him. When the driver opened the narrow, puke-green door, Jeff gasped. There, grinning down at him from the driver's seat, was the skinniest old man the boy had ever seen. The man was so skinny he looked like a skeleton. He wore a weird, old-fashioned uniform that was so strange Jeff wondered if maybe it was a really early Halloween costume.

"Come on up, boy," the driver in the weird get-up called out.

Jeff didn't move. "Thanks, but your bus doesn't go on the route that I need," he said, hoping that he didn't sound as scared as he felt.

"You might be surprised about that, boy," the driver replied in a raspy voice. "Suit yourself. The school year has just started. There's plenty of time yet."

The driver closed the narrow door with a surprisingly loud slam.

Jeff shivered. As the funny-looking bus pulled away, he thought he could see kids sitting inside it. *Probably just reflections on the dirty windows,* Jeff reasoned with a sigh.

Still, he was even more relieved when, a few minutes later, a normal city bus pulled up to the stop. As he got on the white-and-red bus, Jeff showed his transit pass to the normal-looking driver, found a seat and tried not to think about his strange encounter with the old-fashioned bus. By the time he was home, other thoughts had pushed the memory of the spooky old bus and its weird driver right out of the boy's mind.

As a matter of fact, it wasn't until a sunny afternoon early in October that Jeff gave the creepy bus another thought—the very day that same bus pulled up to Jeff's stop again.

That old crate is so weird, Jeff thought. *It must be a special bus because it's not around very often and it really doesn't look as though it belongs here at all.*

The same skinny old driver in the same old uniform opened the bus door for Jeff.

"Hello again, my young friend," the man called out. "Are you ready for a ride on my bus yet?"

Jeff didn't know what to say. He wanted to run back into the school, but running away seemed childish. *This can't be for real. I wish didn't feel scared of him.*

Fighting to make his voice sound less shaky, the boy replied, "No thanks. I'll just wait for my regular bus. It'll be here in a minute."

As Jeff spoke, he tried to peer into the bus. *Are there kids in there or not?* he wondered. *It sort of looks as though there might be, but it's too dark to tell.*

"If I were you I'd take a chance and climb on board. It's getting cold out, you know," the driver responded.

"I'll be fine," Jeff said, stepping even farther back from the curb. *He's right. It is cold, but I don't think riding with him would do much to warm me up.*

"Suit yourself," the man told Jeff. "There's lots of time yet."

Before he steered the bus away, the strange old man threw his head back, opened his mouth wide and let out a laugh that reminded Jeff of a broken

chainsaw cutting through wet wood. The bus door closed and the ugly green vehicle drifted out of sight. The sound of that driver's laugh stayed around longer. It took several minutes for Jeff's apprehension to go away. His mind was so chilled with fright that he didn't even notice when his usual bus pulled up in front of him.

"Hey, kid, wake up!" the driver called, bringing Jeff back to his senses. "Are you getting on or not? I can't wait here all day, y'know."

Embarrassed and still scared, the boy got his bus pass out and stepped onto the regular bus, mumbling his apologies. He settled into his seat and finally began to relax a little.

At least it's warm in here, he thought. *Seeing that green bus today was even scarier than the first time. It's going to take me awhile to forget about that one— especially that dude's horrible laugh.*

Jeff was correct. His second freaky encounter with the strange bus wasn't easy to forget. As a matter of fact, he was still thinking about it when the creepy crate pulled up in front of him one afternoon early in November.

Why does this bus only show up once a month? What route is it on all the other days? Doesn't the

driver get the idea that I'm not going to get on his bus?
Jeff's questions would have gone on, but he realized
that there definitely were kids on the bus—lots of
kids—and every one of their sad, pale faces was
turned toward Jeff.

"Today's the day, I think, my young friend," the
creepy old driver announced to Jeff. "All aboard."

"Not a chance," the terrified boy replied in a shaky
voice. He turned and ran as fast as he could back to
the school.

But when he got there, Jeff felt completely foolish.
*What am I doing? I can hardly tell the principal that a
weird green bus has stopped to pick me up three times
since the new school year began. He'll think I'm nuts!*

Jeff slowly made his way back down to the sidewalk. He had only gone a few steps when the bus he
should've caught drove by without so much as a
moment's pause. *Oh great,* Jeff thought. *Now, on top
of the stupid guy in the green bus completely freaking
me out, I've missed my regular bus. It'll be dark out for
sure by the time I get home.*

Jeff decided to walk home rather than wait for
the next bus to appear. He was still upset about all
that had happened. *I'll be ready for that jerk if he
shows up again next month,* Jeff thought angrily. *I'll*

have a balloon filled with water and ice-chips ready to throw at his bus. That's what I'll do!

Thoughts of the strange green bus, its spooky driver and the pale, sad-looking kids were never far from Jeff's mind after that. Some days he decided that he was going to tell his parents about it. Other days he decided that he had imagined the whole thing.

Before long, his friends noticed changes in the way Jeff was acting. They told him that he was getting weird and that they were going to leave him alone until he decided to get real again. The troubled boy's marks at school dropped, his teachers talked to him about not paying attention in class and then they talked to his parents, who had already scolded him for forgetting to do his chores. In short, the kid's life was a wreck and he was too embarrassed to admit that an old bus was causing all the trouble.

The first Tuesday in December, Jeff had to serve a detention he'd been given for not having his science homework done. It was nearly dark out by the time he left school that day. He made his way to the bus stop, not knowing how long it would be before his bus would arrive. He comforted himself with the thought that at least he was way too late to have to deal with the ugly green bus.

Jeff stood at the bus stop, getting colder and colder with every passing minute. Finally, he saw a familiar-looking bus coming over a rise in the road. He gathered his backpack, took his bus pass out of his pocket and stepped toward the curb, shivering through and through. *It'll be good to get home,* he told himself.

Seconds later, the bus stopped in front of him. That was the good news. The bad news was that it was the horrible ugly old bus again.

"You'd better climb on up this time, lad, or you'll freeze to death standing there," the ghoulish-looking driver in the hideous old uniform called out to Jeff as he cranked the lever to open the bus door.

I'm so cold that even this ugly old guy in his bogus bus looks warm and inviting, Jeff thought, and he climbed on board, holding out his bus pass for the driver to see.

"Gimme that," the driver rasped, showing stubs of rotten teeth.

"What are you doing?" Jeff protested. "Don't put a hole in my bus pass! I need it!"

But even by the time he spoke, Jeff saw that the bus pass already had a star-shaped hole in the upper right-hand corner. He grabbed the pass away from the skinny driver and turned to look for a seat on the bus.

These kids look weird, Jeff thought. *I wonder what school they go to? They all look like death warmed over. It must be one of the schools hit by the flu. That must be why they're so quiet; they're still sick,* Jeff worried as he chose a seat beside the one boy who wasn't quite as pale as the others.

As he sat down, the boy in the next seat glanced over at him. Jeff mumbled "hi" and then turned his head away and closed his eyes. Wrapped in the warmth of the bus, he was just drifting off to sleep when he heard a scratchy voice ask, "Do you like baseball?"

At first Jeff had no idea where the voice came from. Then he turned his head and saw it was the boy beside him who had spoken.

"Oh, sorry," Jeff said. "I guess I must've been falling asleep."

"You *were* asleep. That's why I woke you up. It's not good to fall asleep on *this* bus," the other boy said in a weak voice. "Do you have any baseball cards to trade?"

"Not on me," Jeff lied, thinking the kid was a freak. "I do," the other boy replied. "I bought a pack of bubble gum today, but I knew the card in it wouldn't be any good because the gum was stale. I was right. It was the Jackie Robinson rookie card. That gum must've been at least a year old. Robinson's rookie year was 1947. Besides, I already have one of those. I'll give this one to you if I want."

Jeff felt like an icy snowball had hit him in the back of the neck. He thought the name sounded familiar, that his grandfather had mentioned Jackie Robinson's name. Something about him being the first African-American player in the American League, and being in the Hall of Fame for years and years. His rookie card must be really rare, maybe worth a fortune.

"You have a Jackie Robinson rookie card?" Jeff asked his seatmate.

"Yeah, I guess have two now. The second one's right here. Take it. I really don't want it. I like the pitchers' and catchers' cards best anyway.

Jeff stared in disbelief at the baseball card in his hand. He tried to say "thank you" but words wouldn't come. Suddenly, the boy who'd given him the priceless Jackie Robinson baseball card went completely still and became even paler than the other kids on the bus. As Jeff looked past the boy and out the window, he realized that the bus was not driving on the route to his house. Nothing outside looked familiar at all!

"Hey!" Jeff yelled, grabbing his backpack and hurrying to the bus door. "Let me out!" he screamed at the driver.

The driver let out a menacing laugh—really more of a cackle. "If you wish, my lad," he said stopping the bus and pulling on the crank to open the door.

Jeff jumped to the sidewalk and started to run as soon as his feet hit the pavement. He heard the driver yell after him, "Until next time then, Jeffrey my boy."

Jeff ran as fast as he could for as long as he could. *I'm nowhere near home! I don't recognize anything around here*, the boy thought, and slowed his pace. His heart banged like it was trying to escape from his chest. He stood at an intersection that he didn't recognize, at least not until he looked to his left. *There's the electronics store where Dad bought the computer!*

At last Jeff knew where he was. Home was only a few blocks away. He'd be there in a minute.

When he opened the front door, his mother called out from the kitchen, "Hurry up, Jeff. You're late. We've been holding dinner for you."

The boy smiled and, for the first time since he left school that afternoon, relaxed.

"I'll just put my backpack away," he told his mother as he flung the pack into his room before heading to the dining room. He was so glad to be home that he didn't notice the two small cards that landed on the floor beside his bed. One was a bus pass with a star-shaped hole punched in the top right corner. The other was a baseball card. A Jackie Robinson rookie card.

THE BRIDGE ACROSS TIME

London Bridge is falling down,
falling down, falling down.
London Bridge is falling down,
my fair lady, oh.

That's what the nursery song would have us believe, anyway. Fortunately, the words of the jingle weren't quite true, but by the 1960s the 250-year-old bridge was slowly but surely sinking into England's River Thames. A sinking bridge is not very safe, and so London Bridge was closed. The people in charge wondered what to do next. Making the bridge safe was apparently impossible. Demolishing it wasn't an option either, because London Bridge was a world-famous landmark.

Ideas were proposed and discussed until one enterprising soul made an absolutely ridiculous suggestion. "Let's sell London Bridge!" he suggested. What utter nonsense! Who on earth would buy a sinking bridge? Well, believe it or not, someone did. A man named Robert McCulloch actually bought the famous old structure.

But what would McCulloch do with London Bridge, especially since he lived in Arizona, thousands of miles away from London, England? What's more, Arizona is largely a desert. What could anyone possibly do with a bridge in a desert?

Robert McCulloch was anxious to show the world exactly what could be done with a bridge in a desert. London Bridge would not "fall down"—it would be *taken* down. Brick by brick, English workers took the bridge apart. They numbered each piece carefully so that the workers in Arizona would know how each brick and stone fit together in place. By the time the job was complete, there was no bridge left, just ships full of old, carefully packed, bridge-building material.

Soon, those ships landed at Long Beach, California, which by coincidence is also where the very haunted British ship *Queen Mary* is permanently docked.

From Long Beach, workers transferred the important cargo to trucks that would take the disassembled bridge to its final destination—Lake Havasu in western Arizona.

Many people laughed at Robert McCulloch's crazy and expensive plan, but in the end it was a winner. Careful workers reassembled the bridge like an enormous jigsaw puzzle using the numbers written on the bricks. The entire job took four years. While the workers were busy rebuilding the bridge, other people were also busy in the area. By the time the elegant old bridge stretched across the Arizona lake, an entire village had been built beside it. Robert McCulloch's idea had been a good one. He created a unique tourist attraction—an English village in the American desert. There were double-decker buses, bright red English "call boxes" (we know them as phone booths), pubs and fish-and-chips shops. Now North Americans could experience a bit of Britain without leaving their continent.

In October 1971, the village opened officially. An enormous crowd of people gathered for the ceremony and they watched in awe as four people dressed in old-fashioned British clothing walked slowly across London Bridge. At first, no one paid too much attention to the group on the bridge. Most folks simply assumed that the people in the costumes were actors hired to remind everyone of the famous landmark's heritage. But no actors of any sort had been hired to perform that day.

It wasn't until the group in old-fashioned clothing disappeared before the crowd's eyes that the reality became clear. Robert McCulloch succeeded in importing much more than mortar and bricks to the United States. He also unknowingly brought along some of the many ghosts that have long haunted various parts of London, England.

Today, the bridge remains a successful tourist attraction. It also remains haunted. When spotted, the ghosts on London Bridge seem completely unaware of their modern American surroundings. The apparitions simply stroll along peacefully in their old-fashioned clothing, then vaporize until another day.

THE JACK-O'-LANTERN STORY

Jack-o'-lanterns and Halloween go together like painted eggs and Easter. Have you ever wondered why we carve faces in pumpkins as part of our Halloween celebrations? The answer is an interesting tale and, in part, a ghost story—the story of a ghost doomed to walk the world's paths and trails forever.

Many hundreds of years ago, a man named Jack lived in an Irish village. Jack was not very popular with his neighbors because he was stingy. Jack would take whatever he could without paying for it, and he never offered anything to those in need. As the years went by and Jack got older, he became even more stingy and selfish. The tightfisted man would not share anything with anyone but would always take what was offered to him.

This unpopular fellow also liked to visit the local pub and sip an ice-cold beverage or two. When the other customers saw Stingy Jack coming, they usually scurried for home because he would pester them until they agreed to pay for his drinks.

On top of being miserly, Jack was also not very smart. One day, he invited the devil himself, Satan, to go to the pub with him. Satan accepted the man's invitation and the two enjoyed a drink together.

As usual, when it came time to pay for the drinks, Stingy Jack looked around for someone to help him out. This time, the place was empty. Everyone else had already gone home.

Jack turned to Satan and suggested he turn himself into money. "I'll pay for the drinks that way, my friend," the cheapskate explained. Oddly, the devil agreed.

Not only was Jack stingy and not very bright, but he was also a liar. As soon as Satan turned himself into money, Jack stuffed the coins into his pocket and sneaked away from the pub without paying.

Usually it's tough to feel sorry for Satan, but the poor devil was stuck in Stingy Jack's deep, dark pockets among chunks of lint the size of his big toes. It was disgusting. Worse, Satan needed to get

THE HAUNTED
LADIES

Most of us don't get a chance to ride in big impressive-looking cars that funeral homes have until it's *way* too late to enjoy the ride. Hearses—those dignified vehicles that carry coffins—are very special cars. Usually they're even more luxurious than limousines. Isn't it great, then, that at least one company—one that *isn't* a funeral home—owns two hearses *and* they use them *only* to drive live people around? But best of all, those drives go to and from some of the most haunted places in the world!

The company is Destiny Tours and the haunted places they visit are in and around Sydney, Australia. The funky old hearses are both Cadillacs—one is named Elvira, the other, Morticia. Both of these gorgeous old "ladies" are very haunted, so haunted that they each have a distinct personality! Now that's not something that you can say about most cars, is it?

Elvira is a 1967 model that does not like people standing near her front and "asks" them to move by making them feel very uncomfortable until they finally walk around to her side or back. Morticia, a rare 1962 model, is not air-conditioned, but even so cool breezes blow about inside her on steamy, hot days when her windows are rolled up tight.

As the old funeral cars tour around their wraith-filled routes, they seem to attract lots of other free-floating spirits. There is so much ghostly activity in and around these cars that owner Allan Levinson logs it all in a book.

Allan always knew there was something quite extraordinary about his beloved Elvira. At first he was sure that the car's resident spirit was a mortician named Stan Lance, who had owned the vehicle and who had died five years before. But Mr. Lance rarely drove the car, so Allan began to wonder if another man's spirit haunted his hearse. Not long after that, Debbie Malone, a well-known Australian psychic, revealed that the presence in Allan's car had gone to the spirit world at about the same time as Elvira was "born." Allan knew then that the ghost couldn't be Mr. Lance. Who, then, was it?

It didn't take long to find out.

Mrs. Malone was invited to join the tours, and the gifted woman came away without *any* doubts. She began by announcing, "Morticia and Elvira are definitely haunted." Then she described the supernatural being in Elvira's back seat: a man who wears glasses, a white shirt, black suit and, occasionally, a hat.

Mrs. Malone felt this presence so clearly that she even knew his name—Tom. In all likelihood, Tom was an undertaker who would have loved to drive the hearse when she was new. If people are ever so impolite as to make fun of either Tom or Elvira, they always regret it. Such foolish jokesters almost always come down with an upset stomach—an effective lesson in manners!

Most people, not just psychics or pranksters, feel something *way* out of the ordinary in the car. Sometimes, riders sense the presence of Tom as a dignified, well-dressed man who is very fond of the car. Other times, he makes himself known to passengers as a puzzling pocket of very cold air in the car. Children are generally much better at sensing ghosts than adults are, and so it wasn't much of a shock to

Elvira's driver when an eight-year-old girl declared that she could *see* the cold spot as a white light.

Morticia is a very different "lady," probably because she was not just a hearse but also an ambulance. In addition to carrying dead bodies, she also carried some people who were gravely ill and others who were dying.

Morticia is also haunted by the phantom of a man in uniform. Psychics determined that his name is Bill McGowan and he was a smoker when he was alive. He usually appears in the front, left-hand

seat—where the steering wheel would've been before Morticia was shipped from North America to Australia.

As Elvira and Morticia travel around their spooky routes, the ride can get very "spirited." Other ghosts sometimes join them for part of the trip. When they stop at the old Darlinghurst Gaol (jail) for instance, passengers occasionally feel a strange tightness around their throats. There have been many hangings at that jail over time, which probably explains the uncomfortable feeling around the neck.

Another stop on the tour is a former children's orphanage. Here people often smell roses in the cars, although there are no flowers anywhere near the grand old hearses. After a bit of research, the mystery of the beautiful smell was solved. It seems that an area of the orphanage is haunted by the ghost of a woman who, when she was alive, loved rose-scented perfume.

During one tour, when a group reassembled in Elvira after touring another haunted building, a passenger clearly saw three shadows when there were only two people present at the time. Someone, or something, had obviously decided to tag along for a bit. Another time, a soul from the Woronora Cemetery popped into the hearse after the tour had pulled away from his body's earthly resting-place.

Many folks on these spooky tours like to bring cameras along. Sometimes they are badly disappointed because spirits enjoy messing with people's cameras. Very often, while riding around in either Morticia or Elvira, someone's camera will absolutely refuse to work—for a while. Then, just as suddenly, it will work again perfectly. Apparently, those from beyond don't play with anything for too long before they move on to some other trick. When the cameras do function, the finished pictures usually show round, white dots scattered about. These "orbs" can only be seen on developed film. Most people believe that the orbs are a type of ghostly manifestation.

No doubt by the time you read this, Elvira and Morticia will have even more ghost stories, because Allan Levinson recently explained that on "almost every tour, someone will feel something." So it's possible that while you've been reading about them, the two haunted hearses were showing their passengers a supernaturally good time!

ROAD WRAITH

On a cold, crisp, winter evening some years ago, Joanna and Dan were driving home from a restaurant where they had just enjoyed a fine meal with some friends. The night was clear and beautiful. The moon shone and there was little traffic on the roads. As Dan drove, he and Joanna chatted about the fun they'd had and their plans for the following weekend.

They were driving through an intersection only a few blocks from the restaurant. Suddenly Dan let out a yell, and Joanna jerked her head around to see what the problem was. Then she screamed too, even louder than Dan. But Joanna's scream was drowned out by the sound of their car's tires skidding on the pavement. Dan was almost standing on the brake pedal, his face white with fear. Seconds later, a small black car came speeding across the road. It seemed to be heading straight for them. Bracing themselves for a crash, Dan and Joanna both held their breath until they realized that the other car had missed theirs by a few inches.

"That idiot!" Dan exclaimed. "He didn't even notice that stop sign!"

The couple's happy mood was gone. Dan shook his fist angrily at the dangerous driver who'd nearly hit them. Making rude signals at bad drivers is never a safe thing to do, but Dan was not thinking clearly and didn't realize that his angry gesture would put him and Joanna into the path of grave danger. If he had known, Dan might have used a bit more self-discipline.

It was a few moments before Dan felt calm enough to continue driving. He proceeded through the rest of the intersection slowly and cautiously. He'd driven less than a block when the same car appeared again—right beside his car! The trouble-maker at the wheel of the black car pulled his vehicle up close and waved, hoping that Joanna and Dan had not just seen his car, but had seen him too.

They had!

It was a sight they would never forget. The black car's driver was not a person. It was a skeleton! It stared menacingly at them through empty eye sockets before unlocking its jawbone to laugh madly and silently at the terrified couple.

"Lock your door!" Joanna screamed at Dan, who was concentrating on driving away from the evil black car with its dead driver. No matter how fast Dan drove, the miserable manifestation stayed right beside them!

Finally, almost too terrified to think at all, Dan yelled at Joanna. "Brace yourself!" He yanked the steering wheel sharply to the right. Unfortunately, fear had erased his sense of judgment and their small car smashed hard into the curb.

Now, with a flat tire, a mangled fender and injured pride, Dan's anger had tripled. He looked around for the deadly driver who had caused the accident, but the street was deserted.

"That's ridiculous!" Dan growled. "He couldn't have driven away from us that quickly. His car was right beside ours just a second ago."

Joanna reached over and put her hand on Dan's arm. "Forget about the stupid car. So long as it's gone, then I'm happy. Who cares where or how it got away? We're lucky that all we need is a tow truck, not an ambulance. Or a hearse."

Dan didn't reply. He took his cell phone out of his shirt pocket and called for road service.

By the time the tow truck arrived, Dan and Joanna had climbed out of their car to lean against its fender. They stood upright and moved toward the tow-truck driver as he got out of his truck.

"How did you manage this?" the tow-truck driver asked.

Dan replied, "You're not going to believe this—it's going to sound a little crazy, but a maniac driver with the best skeleton costume I've ever seen is to blame for this."

The tow-truck driver gaped at them.

"You must mean the phantom car!" he exclaimed. "I can hardly believe it. As far as I know, no one's seen that evil thing for years! That's no Halloween costume the driver's wearing—that's him—he's a skeleton—a phantom skeleton. His car's a phantom too. The folks around here call it 'the car from hell.'" He walked around the car, assessing the damage. "From all I've heard, I guess they have good reason to call it that. Listen, I think you can drive your car if we just change the tire. If you want, I can tell you the legend while I'm changing the tire for you."

Both Joanna and Dan nodded and moved to the front of their car.

"Hand me a wrench," the tow-truck driver said, pointing to a toolbox he'd set down on the curb. "I'll have this flat tire changed and you'll be on your way again in a few minutes."

"Not till you explain what just happened," Joanna reminded him.

"Oh yes, the phantom car," the man said as he went right to work. "They say it was first seen about 25 years ago, the very night that they pulled a small black car up from the bottom of the harbor. The paramedics and police said the car must have been under the water for months—with the driver's body still in it. They said that it looked as though the fish had fed on every bit of flesh the man ever had. According to the news, there was nothing left of him at all. Nothing except his bones, of course."

The tow-truck driver stood up, wiped his hands on a rag that he'd had in his pocket and began to pick up the tools he'd used to change the damaged tire.

"For years afterward, the image of that car and its driver were seen around here, but then talk about the 'car from hell' pretty much died down. You two are the first folks I've heard about in years who've seen it. Guess you found out why they call it 'the car from hell.'"

After paying the man for changing their tire, Dan and Joanna carefully drove back home. There was no more happy chatter between them. The only time they spoke was when they agreed not to mention their supernatural encounter with the phantom "car from hell" to anyone. Ever.

We should hope that Dan and Joanna never visit Bachelor's Grove Cemetery near Chicago, Illinois. Phantom cars and even phantom trucks are regularly seen driving near the graveyard. Most of the ghostly vehicles look as though they're from the 1930s. People say that these phantoms are the ghosts of cars and trucks once owned by some of Chicago's worst gangsters.

So, next time you're out driving with your parents, or even crossing the street, don't be too sure that the cars you're seeing are real—they may be road wraiths!

HAILED FROM BEYOND

Liverpool, England, is famous for being The Beatles' hometown, but it is also the hometown to thousands of ghosts. Some of the ghost stories go back several hundred years but others, like the next tale, are much more recent.

In the mid-1990s, a young man named Brian decided that he wanted to be a taxi cab driver. To do that, he needed to take special driving lessons, pass a test for cab drivers and buy a taxi. Brian placed an ad in the local newspaper. The very next day a man named Alan called him. Alan, it seemed, was a neighbor who had driven cabs for years but was anxious to get out of that business and into an office job. The two arranged to meet so that Brian could try out the car. After a quick test drive and a brief conversation, the two men struck a deal and Brian bought the cab from Alan at an affordable price.

Alan and Brian were both delighted. For a while.

The night Brian took the car out for his first shift, he was just as proud as could be. Those guys from high school who used to tease him because he couldn't play football would be envious now! He owned a jet-black, clean, shiny taxi. This was a moment to be treasured! Besides, from now on, the harder he worked, the more money he would make. He could soon be rich. Since he loved driving anyway, the whole arrangement seemed perfect, almost too good to be true.

The evening started well, and pleasant passengers left him generous tips. By the time the cab company's dispatcher called to tell him to pick up a rider from an address on Pinehurst Road in a nearby suburb, Brian was feeling terrific about himself and his new career.

As Brian drove away from the city's downtown area, he passed fewer and fewer tall buildings. He was thoroughly enjoying himself and even wondered if perhaps this sort of trip, just a bit out of town, would eventually become his favorite. Just as that thought struck him, the car began to slow down. *Odd*, Brian thought, *I wasn't easing up on the gas pedal.* He pressed his foot down more firmly. The car suddenly went faster, and the steering wheel spun hard to the left. The hard and fast turn threw Brian across the car's seat.

"Whoa!" he yelled. He had been knocked so far over that he banged his head on the rearview mirror.

The pit of his stomach heaved with that horrible sick feeling you get when something awful has just happened. For a moment, Brian thought he might throw up, and he grabbed the steering wheel even harder. He fought to straighten the car while pulling himself back behind the wheel. He managed to steer safely over to the side of the road. He needed a moment to calm down. His forehead stung where he'd banged it, the palms of his hands were slippery with sweat and he had goosebumps all up and down his arms.

A few minutes later, Brian was calm enough to drive again, but he steered away from the curb very slowly to make sure that the car was running properly. Everything seemed to be working just fine, he decided, but he wasn't completely reassured. He knew that what had just happened was a very bad sign, and he was worried.

As he drove along, nearing the address where he was to pick up his passenger, Brian began to calm down. *Maybe it was just my imagination,* he thought. *Or maybe I've been so excited that I got a little light headed. The car's probably fine. Alan wouldn't have sold it to me if it had been dangerous.*

For a second, he remembered the low price he'd paid for the nearly new vehicle, but he pushed that suspicion out of his mind. Such thoughts were a distraction and he was a cab driver with a passenger waiting to be picked up.

He drove slowly until he saw the name of the road where he wanted to turn right. As he approached the intersection, Brian put his right turn signal on and adjusted his hands on the wheel. As he did, the car turned left again! This time, the young man was able to hold himself in place so that he didn't bang his head again, but his stomach filled with what seemed like ice cubes as he realized that he was not the one controlling the car. Something or someone that he could not see and did not understand was in charge.

What kind of sick joke is this? Brian was no longer worried about finding Pinehurst Road and his passenger. *I'm heading back into the city now! And the first thing I'm going to do is talk to Alan. He has some explaining to do!*

As Brian grasped the steering wheel and turned the car around on the street, he glanced into the rearview mirror to make sure the road behind him was clear. For an awful second, all he could see reflected back at him was a portion of his own face. He jumped in fear, but then remembered that he had bumped up against the mirror pretty hard. He probably knocked the thing sideways. He raised his shaky hand to adjust the mirror's cold metal frame. It was angled down now, down to the floor beside him.

A scream rose in Brian's throat and then escaped as a moan at the sight of a pair of men's shoes beside his own. Worse, those shoes were attached to a man's legs, clad in dark pants.

As he twisted the mirror farther, Brian could see a dark jacket over a vest and a shirt so white it sparkled. A black bow tie was centered on the shirt's collar. Above that collar was a head with a bearded face. The face shimmered like millions of tiny pinpricks of light. Brian looked in the mirror again, hoping that the car's floor would be empty this time. Perhaps the mirror had broken when he hit it and perhaps it was no longer reflecting the way it should.

But it was hopeless. As he struggled to breathe, Brian realized he had bought a haunted taxicab!

Fear pumped through his body, deep and painful, but he could not make himself look away. As Brian watched in amazement, the specter lowered his chin to his chest and began to disappear, ever so slowly.

Once again Brian found himself alone in the car. When he was able to control his shaking hands, he drove away. By the time he'd reached Alan's house, his fear had been replaced by pure white anger at the rotten neighbor who sold him a haunted cab without even a hint about its problem.

Alan opened the front door of his house when he saw Brian coming up the walk. "I'm sorry, my friend," were his first words. "I can see that you've found out my secret. I should've told you. I am sorry, really I am."

Still in shock, Brian stood in silence, listening to the other man's apologies. Alan continued, "There's nothing wrong with the car. Not mechanically, that is. It's definitely haunted, though."

"Then that *was* a ghost I saw, wasn't it? I was right, wasn't I? That was a ghost?" Brian said.

"Yes," Alan began. "That's why I was so eager to get rid of the taxi. Just over a week ago, I picked that man up and he asked me to take him to an address in the suburbs. He said it was his home. He looked very sick and I told him that he should go to the hospital, not home."

With his dying breaths, the man had protested, "I must go home. I am very sick. I'm dying. I must go home to die."

Alan looked at Brian, then continued. "Poor soul didn't make it. I tried to drive as quickly as I could while still keeping an eye on him but, just a block later, I saw his head fall on to his chest. Seconds later, he passed from this world to the next. Since then, his phantom has appeared in the car every now and again. I think it happens mostly when the car is around the area of Pinehurst Avenue."

Brian interjected immediately. "No, you mean Pinehurst Road. That's where I was going. To Pinehurst Road."

"Pinehurst Road, Pinehurst Avenue, what difference does it make? All I know is that the ghost only appears in the car at that one location."

"I'll tell you what the difference is, you fool!" Brian shouted. "Obviously the man lived on Pinehurst Road. You were taking him to Pinehurst Avenue. It was the wrong place! The poor soul is still trying to get home!"

"Well, it doesn't matter much now, does it?" Alan said. "He's dead. It'll probubly never happen again. Hey, let me tell you about this great welding business I'm buying into. The shop's almost new, and the equipment is all good quality. If you're not going to drive a cab, maybe this'll work for you. The price is almost too good to be true! What do you think? Are you interested?"

Brian stumbled away from Alan's house and into the street, still in shock over his experience with the phantom in the taxi and angry with Alan's response. The next day he sold the cab. Brian never did explain why he sold the car for such a low price, but he did warn the buyer not to take the car out of the downtown area.

To my knowledge, that cab is still being driven around the streets of Liverpool. There haven't been any more reports of ghostly sightings, but that doesn't put the paranormal matter to rest. Perhaps the ghost hasn't reappeared because no one has driven it near the dead man's home. Or it could simply be that no one who has since witnessed this haunting ever spoke of it. Or maybe the dead man's soul finally found its way home.

SUPERNATURAL SIMILARITIES

On April 10, 1912, a huge and luxurious ship called the *Titanic* set out from England on its first and only voyage across the Atlantic Ocean to New York. The *Titanic*'s owners were so sure that their beautiful new vessel would be a success that they had already started to build another one just like it. They called these two magnificent ships "floating palaces" and declared that sailing across the Atlantic would never be the same again. Henceforth, the voyage would be a long, elegant party for anyone rich enough to afford to travel first-class.

Experts assured the passengers that the *Titanic* was not only grand, but absolutely safe. "This ship is unsinkable," they claimed. Wealthy people from all over the world could hardly wait to buy their expensive tickets to sail away on this grand ship's very first trip.

As you know, the *Titanic*'s voyage ended in tragedy. On April 14, 1912, its crew either didn't see or didn't report a mountain of ice in front of the ship until it was too late to avoid a collision. The ship sank, taking 1522 people to the bottom of the North Atlantic.

A man named Morgan Robertson was not surprised by the terrible tragedy. Fourteen years before the *Titanic* sank, Robertson had a vivid and detailed nightmare. In his terrible dream, a huge and luxurious ship, filled with wealthy passengers, sank in freezing water during the month of April. The name of the ship in Robertson's nightmare was the *Titan*. Robertson's dream was so clear that he wrote down every detail of it and later published the story as a book.

In 1912, as soon as Robertson heard about the wonderful new *Titanic,* he realized that it was almost identical, even in name, to the ship he'd dreamed and written about. What should he do? Robertson thought about warning the *Titanic*'s owners of the scary similarities between the real ship and his dream ship, but he was afraid that they would think he was crazy. So Robertson did nothing. Maybe he was correct, and the *Titanic's* owners would have laughed at him for comparing their wonderful new vessel to a mere bad dream. We'll never know.

In another strange twist, in 1930, less than 20 years after the *Titanic* sank, people actually bragged about large and luxurious type of "airship" being "like the *Titanic.*" The British company that built this dirigible, or blimp, named it the *R101* and described it as "the *Titanic* of the air."

You've likely seen blimps on television during sporting events like football games. They often carry advertisements for tires on their sides, and they show viewers what the sports field looks like from high above. These "airships" are big oblong balloons, each with a large basket hanging beneath it. Today's blimps hold only a few people, but in 1930 the "basket" underneath the enormous *R101* was more like a small hotel, big enough to transport dozens of people.

By comparing the *R101* to the doomed ship *Titanic,* the owners of the aircraft were trying to tell people that the blimp would be the most luxurious way for rich people to travel. And like the *Titanic's* builders, the owners of the *R101* had complete confidence in their craft's safety. Instead of proclaiming that their "ship" was unsinkable, they advertised it as being "as safe as a house."

As with the *Titanic*, the *R101* crashed on its first-ever trip, mostly as a result of the crew not paying enough attention. But although no one has ever admitted to having a *nightmare* about the *R101* like Morgan Robertson had about the *Titan*, a psychic named Eileen Garrett "saw" the deadly crash of a dirigible in 1926, before the *R101* had even been built.

At the time, Garrett did nothing about her sighting because no one knew that such a craft would ever be built. Two years later, though, Garrett had a second psychic sighting about the deadly accident and contacted Sir Sefton Brancker, the government official responsible for the project. The man ignored her warning and had workers carry on building the *R101*. In 1929, Garrett had a third psychic sighting of the blimp. This time she saw the airship falling from the sky with flames surrounding it. Perhaps because no one had paid any attention to her previous message, Eileen Garrett did not tell anyone of her third vision.

In October 1930, her predictions came true. On its first-ever voyage, the *R101* crashed in France, killing 48 of its 52 passengers, including Brancker.

A few days after the deadly *R101* accident, Eileen Garrett conducted a séance to communicate with the spirits who died in the crash. The ghost of the *R101*'s captain made his presence known first, and gave details about the blimp and its crash that only its captain would know. When newspaper reporters heard about the captain's soul returning to this world, they were fascinated and began writing stories about Eileen Garrett's psychic abilities.

In all, the woman held seven séances to find out all she could about *R101*'s terrible failure. Several of those killed in the crash, including Sir Sefton Brancker, the man who disregarded Garrett's warnings about the *R101*, came back to explain that the crash had been caused by a gas leak, which had sparked a fire. Her vision of flames shooting from the blimp had been 100 percent accurate.

A word of advice: turn down any invitation you receive to travel on anything ever compared to either the *Titanic* or the *R101*. For our own safety, it's probably best to pay attention to warnings from "the other side."

FAMOUS PHANTOM TRAIN

It was twilight—that strange time that is neither day nor night. Jim glanced at his watch, which read 7:20. He'd have to head home soon.

It's so cold, the 13-year-old boy thought as he sat on the top ledge of a frosty wooden fence. *It's April but it feels more like winter.* Jim pumped his legs back and forth at a steady pace and crossed his arms over his chest to try to keep his long, lanky body warm. Despite being uncomfortably chilly, Jim enjoyed being outside and by himself at one of his favorite places.

The fence along the south boundary of his family's property was near the rail line, and Jim loved to stare along the empty miles of tracks. The view somehow made him feel that the whole world stretched out endlessly before him. Breathing in the crisp, unseasonably cold air seemed to sharpen his thinking. Maybe he'd be able to plan his pitching strategy for his next baseball game.

Jim checked his watch for a second time and eased himself down from his perch. *It's wicked how cold it is out here,* he thought. *I'd better get home.*

Just as Jim was about to take his first stride toward home, a noise stopped him. It was an odd sound, and it came from way off in the distance. As he paused to listen, he got colder and colder and also a bit worried. Thick pillows of gray fog rose from the ground in front of him. Within seconds Jim was wrapped in silent, murky blackness. *It's so dark. It's pitch black and way too quiet, like something's absorbed every little bit of light and sound in the world,* Jim thought.

A cold, hard shudder snaked down the boy's backbone. *I can't even see the train tracks,* Jim realized. The coppery taste of panic filled the back of his throat. Jim tried to flee toward the warmth and safety of home, but his feet seemed frozen to the ground. *Fog can't paralyze a person, can it?* he wondered before reality hit him. That weird sound he had heard was really not a sound at all. It was the exact opposite—it was silence. Total silence. Silence every bit as thick and gray and dense as the spine-chilling fog shapes surrounding him.

Dark clouds above him blacked out the last thin, watery ribbon of moonlight. Jim's body sagged. Everything he counted on in his world was gone. He was beyond frightened.

The dark, silent stillness hung about him for just a moment longer. Then, through the thick blanket of fog, Jim saw something even darker. It was a solid black shape and it was moving toward him along the tracks. Seconds later, Jim saw an enormous locomotive. Slowly, but steadily, the train engine made its way through the fog.

Another shudder wracked his body as the mammoth locomotive passed directly in front of him. It was at least twice as big as any Jim had ever seen. The engine was covered with pieces of black cloth that fluttered like flags on a blustery day.

Jim glanced down at the tracks—tracks that he thought he knew so well. Much to his horror, the boy realized they were no longer made of steel. Instead, this unnatural train was traveling over a black carpet spread endlessly out in front of it. Looking up again,

Jim found he could see inside the train cars as they rolled past him. Right behind the locomotive was another huge railcar. It too was draped in black and utterly silent. Inside, an assortment of soldiers stood at attention around a table. They wore strange-looking, old-fashioned uniforms and were not quite life-like. Atop the table lay a coffin. The car following carried some sort of an orchestra—musicians that almost, but not quite, looked like flesh-and-blood human beings. Each spectral musician wore black. The bizarre train carrying a coffin, wraith-like soldiers and images of musicians rolled past Jim in deadly silence.

That's an old-fashioned steam engine! Jim realized. *I've seen models of them. This can't be real. Locomotives make noise, lots of noise. This can't be happening.*

But it was.

Jim watched as the supernatural vision slowly and silently disappeared into the distance. *The train must've taken the fog with it,* Jim thought.

His world returned to normal. The temperature seemed to get warmer and the clouds even cleared. Jim sighed with relief as he found he was able to move once again. *I'd better get home! It must be really late. And I sure can't tell Mom that I was watching a ghost train pass by!*

Jim looked down at his watch—it was eight minutes *before* the freaky train came through the fog! *But that's impossible!* Jim thought. *That train took at least 20 minutes to pass. Or at least it seemed to.*

An icicle of terror dripped down Jim's spine. He sprinted away from the tracks as fast as his frightened legs would carry him.

Jim's house seemed an especially warm and welcoming place that night! He still had no idea what he'd encountered down by the railroad tracks. He was just relieved that his strange adventure had ended and that he was safely back home!

What a shame that young Jim hadn't known that he had witnessed one of the world's most famous and enduring ghostly events. He had seen the phantom of President Abraham Lincoln's funeral train, which in April 1865 carried the president's body back to his home in Springfield, Illinois.

Every April, along the route that the slain president's funeral train traveled those many, many years ago, there are reports of supernatural images like the one Jim encountered. As a matter of fact, so many people have seen President Lincoln's phantom train that the spectral spectacle has been reported in newspapers and magazines around the world. For instance, as long ago as 1872, just seven years after President Lincoln was assassinated, a newspaper reporter noted that the ghost train is seen regularly in the month of April. The air on the track becomes very keen and cutting. Soon after, the engine with long black streamers and a band with black instruments pass noiselessly. The very air grows black.

If it is moonlight, clouds always come over the moon and the music seems frozen by horror. A few moments after that, the phantom train with the murdered Lincoln's body aboard glides by. The wind, if blowing, dies away at once and overall there is a solemn hush. Clocks and watches always stop and when looked at again are found to be five to eight minutes behind.

But what of the silence? How could a train pass any spot without making a noise? Surely that is impossible. For a normal train, yes, of course, silence *is* completely impossible. But a phantom train's noise is apparently drowned out by supernatural silence.

If you'd like to see this important paranormal moment in America's history yourself, your best bet is to watch carefully near train tracks in certain northern states on the evening of April 20.

HAUNTED HANGAR

When cars are not in use, they're stored in garages. But where do airplanes go when they're not flying? Usually they're kept in huge garage-type buildings called "hangars."

Perhaps its size makes an airplane hangar a spooky place, especially when it's empty. A hangar is so big that every footstep, every word and every creak echoes for long time. Or perhaps an airplane hangar might feel spooky for another reason. Perhaps, like Hangar 43 at an airport in Kansas, it may be haunted.

The "facts" surrounding this haunted hangar story from Kansas have become a bit muddled over the 50 or so years a ghost has lived in Hangar 43, but it's still a very intriguing tale.

One version of this ghost story tells us that the phantom who haunts Hangar 43 is the spirit of a young pilot killed when his plane crashed into a nearby airport building. The folks who believe in him usually refer to the ghost as "Captain." Another version of the tale tells us that the hangar's resident wraith is not the spirit of a pilot at all, but the ghost of a maintenance worker killed when he fell from a platform high up near the ceiling of the huge building.

Although there may be some disagreement about who the ghost is, there is no doubt that the hangar is haunted. The ghost is rarely seen, but many folks have witnessed his actions. For instance, the spirit is generally blamed when people see water faucets turn on and off by themselves. And when doors open and close in an empty area of the big building, most witnesses presume that the ghost has just walked from one room to another.

This well-accepted ghost, whoever he might be, seems to be a happy soul. People who work at this Kansas airport often report hearing cheery whistling and phantom footsteps that stride across a platform up near the ceiling of the haunted hangar. When workers hear the ghost walking and whistling they usually just smile and accept that the entity is simply living his afterlife. He doesn't even seem to be aware that he lived a long time ago.

Once, though, while a group of workers played cards during a lunch break, a coffee mug on their table lifted a few inches from the table-top and then turned itself upside down, spilling coffee all over! That time, the card players definitely felt that their invisible work-mate had gone too far!

It's a good thing that the ghost doesn't pull pranks very often because it seems that he doesn't want to leave Hangar 43. At last report, almost everyone agreed that the ghost had not yet left the building.

BOGUS BUS TO BLAME

Tales about phantom buses are not uncommon, perhaps because buses (both phantom and real) generally travel over and over again along busy routes that lots of people use. There are even reports of a police officer chasing a spectral bus through a red light, thinking that the vehicle had broken the law. It's difficult to imagine whether the officer was relieved or upset to learn that he or she had been trying to ticket a driver who had been dead for years!

Fortunately, stories about ghost buses causing trouble in the here and now *are* uncommon, but some records of such strange events do exist.

One of the best-documented cases of a phantom bus causing a real collision was reported in London, England, in 1934 when a young man was driving his car through an intersection. He noticed a bus moving toward him so fast that it seemed a collision was imminent. In a frantic attempt to avoid a crash, the young driver twisted his car's steering wheel as hard as he could. The move sent his car straight into the path of another automobile. The two cars collided, making a screeching noise and scattering broken bits of metal and glass all around.

At the exact moment that the two cars hit, people nearby also watched a bus travel straight through the accident scene. Afterward, many of them commented that the bus seemed to glide through the smashed cars as though it wasn't quite solid.

Investigators later discovered that a phantom bus was often seen crossing the street at that very spot!

GUARDIAN GHOSTS

This ghostly tale is especially close to my heart because it happened to an old friend of mine. The story begins on December 29, 1972. An airplane was approaching its final destination of Miami, Florida. Flight 401 was almost over.

Captain Bob, First Officer Albert and Second Officer Dan were busy preparing for the landing when they noticed a small red indicator light flashing on the cockpit's control panel. It was the warning light for the plane's landing gear. At first, the pilots were not concerned because the type of airplane they were flying was so reliable. Even so, a light was flashing and that meant that the situation had to be checked out.

Dan volunteered to squeeze into the small space below the cockpit where he could see if the plane's wheels were still up or whether they were lowered, locked in place and ready to touch down on the runway. Tragically, as the three experienced flyers discussed and investigated the possible problem with the landing gear, they were not paying attention to guiding the plane safely into the airport and, as a result, the jet headed toward the earth like a bullet out of a gun.

Seconds later, the plane crashed.

Seventy souls survived that terrible accident, but more than 100 did not. Captain Bob and Second Officer Dan were among those killed.

A heart-wrenching rescue and clean-up operation began almost immediately after the crash. When it was all over, the experts involved determined that some of the parts from the wrecked plane hadn't been damaged, but were still in good condition and could be used in other planes. For example, kitchen equipment from the downed plane was installed in another jet that needed new ovens. The company's recycling idea seemed like a good way to save money. No one predicted what would happen next.

Flight attendants working on planes now containing parts from the crashed aircraft soon began seeing Bob and Dan riding along on their flights. Of course, they all knew that both pilots were dead and it could only mean one thing. The images they were seeing were ghosts! The souls of the captain and the second officer were haunting the planes that had acquired parts from Flight 401.

My friend Anna was the first one to tell me about these ghosts. She'd worked as a flight attendant for many years and was very familiar with her job. But nothing had prepared her for what she saw one evening while she was making coffee in a plane's kitchen. Anna was busy at a small counter with a set of small ovens behind her. As she turned around she nearly dropped a tray of full coffee cups. There, reflected in the glass door of one of the ovens, was the clear image of Second Officer Dan's face!

Anna was utterly stunned. Fortunately, she had already heard many of the rumors about these guardian ghosts haunting particular planes. Once she'd gotten over the shock of seeing one, Anna actually felt comforted. She recognized Dan's face immediately. She smiled at the image, nodded and went on about her work. She was sure that the second officer's spirit would protect the flight because she knew the ghost had once told a pilot, "There will never be another crash of [a plane like this]. We will not let it happen."

Anna's encounter was not the only one to occur in an airplane's kitchen. On another occasion, Dan's conscientious spirit was seen repairing a possible problem with an aircraft. As soon as he was finished the work his image vanished.

Dan's spirit once appeared to warn of a possible mechanical problem with a plane. The crew took the ghost's presence seriously enough to land at the next airport and have the plane thoroughly checked. Sure enough, its engine needed to be repaired. The problem may not have been spotted if it hadn't been for a warning from the other side.

Dan's visits to our time and place are not always for such dramatic reasons, but he does usually want to help. Much to the amazement of the flesh-and-blood workers on other flights, the second officer's specter has done routine checks and has even made announcements! The only time he did not bring ghostly assistance was when his apparition, still dressed in his airline uniform, sat beside an unsuspecting female passenger. When the woman tried to make conversation with the former second officer, it became obvious that her seatmate was not human. As she and a flight attendant watched in horror, the ghost vanished before their eyes.

The captain's phantom has not been seen as frequently as Dan's, but he was seen just before take-off sitting quietly on a plane as though he was a passenger. Of course, the crew working that day recognized Bob, who had been dead for many months by that time, so they knew they were seeing a ghost. When his presence was approached, the entity dissolved into thin air! The people who had seen the deceased captain were so shaken by the encounter that the flight was cancelled entirely.

Not long after these supernatural encounters, airline employees began to wonder why some planes were haunted, but others were not. The answer was simple. It seemed that the apparitions were only ever seen onboard planes with one or more of Flight 401's salvaged parts. The souls of the dead men had stayed with their airplane—all parts of it!

Of course with all these ghost-sighting reports, it was not long before executives with the company that owned the haunted airplanes became aware of the helpful ghosts. Now the executives had no choice. The hauntings had to be reported to aviation authorities. Not surprisingly, the stories about the ghosts were publicly denied, but at least the encounters were officially recorded.

By now, this particular aircraft model is no longer flown—for reasons that have nothing to do with either the ghosts or the hauntings. That type of plane is simply too big and uses too much fuel.

Let's hope that the spirits of both Captain Bob and Second Officer Dan have also retired—to their eternal reward.

USED CAR WITH EXTRAS

When Janice Stevenson graduated from high school, she and her parents agreed that she would need her own car. The college she was planning to attend the following September was several miles from home and a bus route did not link the two.

Janice and her father spent every Saturday morning in July shopping for a good used car that didn't cost too much money. Finally, they found an old sedan for sale at a reasonable price. It seemed to be the perfect car for a first-year college student. Janice was delighted and her father was relieved. The next morning, the used car was parked in front of the Stevensons' house.

Before noon that day, Janice had already phoned her three closest friends. She was excited about her car and wanted to show it off, so she invited them to go for a drive with her after dinner that day. She decided to wash the car before picking the girls up, since she wanted it to look its best when they saw it.

Right after lunch, Janice prepared a bucket of warm, sudsy water and unraveled the garden hose. She started by washing the roof of her new car. Next, she soaked down its trunk and hood. With each wipe of the soapy sponge across car's paint, the young woman was more excited about it. Then, as she pulled the hose around the car so she could clean the passenger's side, Janice stopped dead in her tracks. There in the passenger's door was a row of tiny holes. She hadn't noticed them before.

The holes were too small to ruin the look of the car, but something about them made Janice feel very uncomfortable, even frightened. For a moment, she couldn't even move. She finally told herself that she was just acting silly. Holes in a car door couldn't possibly hurt her! Still, she had to take some deep breaths before she could force herself to move closer to the car. She reached out and felt the strange trio of marks on the door.

I wonder if this is what bullet holes look like, she thought as a film of cold sweat began to form on her skin. *I'm not telling Dad—he'd just worry. It's a good car and I'm lucky to have it.*

Janice dipped her sponge back into the bucket and discovered that her wash water had suddenly turned cold. She hurried to finish the job.

By the time she left that evening to pick up her friends, Janice had forgotten all about the marks on her car door. Soon, she and Diane, Christine and Melanie were out for their first-ever drive together in Janice's new car. They were chatting and laughing and thoroughly enjoying themselves when Melanie, who was sitting in the backseat next to Diane, suggested stopping at a convenience store for a cold drink.

"Great idea!" the others chorused.

Janice turned the steering wheel toward the store's parking lot. As she did, Christine screamed and grabbed Janice's arm.

"Stop it, Chris!" Janice screamed back. "I can't drive when you're pulling at me."

Those words were no sooner out of her mouth than she realized her friend *needed* to grab onto her. The passenger's side door had flown open. Christine would have fallen out of the car if she hadn't been able to grab onto Janice.

"Are you all right?" Janice asked as she slowed the car to a stop in the parking lot. Christine didn't answer. She just sat there, still clutching Janice. Both girls were shaken over the incident. Diane and Melanie leaned forward to see if anyone in the front seat had been hurt. For a while, no one said a word. Finally, in a quiet, crackly sort of a voice, Janice managed to utter, "I guess the door must be broken. I'm so sorry, Chris. I had no idea."

"It's okay, I guess," the shivering teen answered as she pried her fingers from the arm of Janice's jacket. "I'm not hurt."

"Maybe we should forget about the soft drinks and just head home," Diane suggested. "Christine can sit in the back with us on the way there."

The passengers rearranged themselves and Janice, scared and disappointed, began the drive back to their neighborhood.

"You're home a lot earlier than we expected you to be," Janice's mother commented when the girl came in the house.

For a moment, Janice considered explaining what happened to ruin their evening, but then thought better of it. *Dad'll feel terrible if he thinks he chose a bad car for me. Chris is a scatterbrain, anyway. She probably didn't close the door properly in the first place.*

"We just decided to make it an early evening, Mom," Janice replied, not really telling a lie. "I'm going up to bed now."

The next day, Janice's mother asked her to run an errand. "Now that you have your own car, I can count on you for more help!" her mother added with a smile.

A little nervous, Janice climbed into the car and drove to the city's business district. All went well. The car ran smoothly and all the doors stayed closed. Janice concluded that Chris couldn't have closed the door tightly enough the night before. She felt much happier and more confident by the time she started her drive home. And the closer she got to her own neighborhood, the better she felt. In fact, when she was just a block from home, she considered phoning her friends again to ask them out for a proper drive that night.

Too busy thinking about her friends, Janice didn't hear the strange sound coming from the car seat beside her. She didn't notice anything until she turned the corner toward her street and the passenger door flew open again!

Slamming on the brakes, Janice reached across the car seat toward the open door. Unfortunately, she took her hands off the steering wheel. The car hit the curb with a thump and came to a stop. Janice wasn't really hurt but she was badly shaken. A neighbor had heard the car smack into the curb, and he ran out of his house to see what was wrong.

By then, of course, her secret about the door not staying closed was as good as out. The man who came to help knew the Stevenson family well. In a matter of moments, her parents would know there was a problem with the car.

The man helped Janice out of the car and walked her home. He told her parents how the car door had flown open when Janice turned the corner. The next day, Mr. Stevenson drove the car to a repair shop where he and a mechanic thoroughly inspected the door's hinges and lock. Together the two spent over an hour looking for the problem that was causing the door to swing open, but they never found it. They did, however, see the three tiny holes in the outside of the faulty door.

"Those are bullet holes," the mechanic exclaimed.

As the color drained from his face, Janice's father slowly nodded his head in agreement. A moment later he said, "This is not the car for my daughter. There's definitely something not right about it. Frankly, I think the place for this car is at the auto wrecker's. It needs to be destroyed."

With that, Mr. Stevenson borrowed a length of rope from the mechanic's garage. He rolled down the passenger's window and wound the rope round and round the doorframe, tying the door closed. Then, with a sigh, he climbed behind the wheel and drove to an auto wrecker's yard on the south side of town.

He was almost there when he turned onto a street that led past Pleasantview Cemetery. Suddenly, without warning and despite the rope holding it closed, the car's passenger door flew open. The rope that should have kept it closed was gone—likely lying on the road near the cemetery. Mr. Stevenson didn't bother with it. He just kept his hand on the passenger door handle and somewhat awkwardly drove the rest of the way to the auto wrecker's yard.

An old man wearing striped overalls and a greasy scarf around his neck came through the gate at the entrance.

"Good morning," he greeted Mr. Stevenson. "Got a car there for me, do you?"

"I'm afraid so," Mr. Stevenson replied. "It needs to be destroyed. I bought it for my daughter but it's just not safe enough for her. It's not safe enough for anyone, I guess."

"That one again?" the wrecker croaked in his odd voice. "I already flattened that car once. It was just a few months ago, right after it'd been involved in that shooting at the convenience store. Some punks shot at the passenger while the car was stopped in a parking lot. As far as I know, the bullets were still lodged in the door when I wrecked it. The guy was killed instantly. As a matter of fact, he's buried just over there in Pleasantview Cemetery."

Mr. Stevenson took a cab home.

Janice bought her grandmother's used car. It had no holes and its doors only opened when they were supposed to.

A MODEL RESCUE

In the autumn of 1955, 11-year-old Rick felt as though his entire world had fallen apart. Rick's grandfather, whom the boy admired more than anyone else in the world, had just died. Grandpa had been an airline pilot—which was what Rick dreamed of becoming when he grew up. But now, without the older man to teach him, the boy worried that he would no longer be able to reach his lifelong goal.

For months after his grandfather's death, Rick felt horribly sad. He missed Grandpa terribly and continued to worry that now he would never be able to sit in the cockpit of a plane. As winter came and went, nothing succeeded in lifting the boy's spirits. It wasn't until his 12th birthday the following April that Rick finally began to feel happier.

Rick's parents gave him a model airplane, the kind that really flies, as a birthday gift. When he opened the package and saw the plane, Rick finally felt happy again—happier than he'd been since his grandfather's death. The model plane was a beauty, and realistic enough to remind Rick why he'd always wanted to fly.

Of course, Rick received other birthday presents that day, but once he'd seen the model, all he wanted to do was to get outside and see his new plane fly. After he'd eaten too many hot dogs and far too much birthday cake, Rick was allowed to go out to play. But just as the excited boy was about to walk out the back door, his mother added, "Don't go near the quarry. Oh, and take John with you."

John was Rick's nine-year-old brother. There wasn't anything wrong with him except that he was a kid. Rick was about to protest that it was *his* birthday and so he shouldn't have a kid tagging along with him, but when he saw the look on his little brother's face, Rick realized that John really wanted to come along.

"Yeah, sure," he said and held the door open for the smaller boy. Their mother reminded them about the quarry *every* time they went out to play, as if they might have forgotten about the abandoned marble quarry less than half a mile from their house. None of the kids in town was allowed anywhere near the old excavation. Only the dumbest ones ever disobeyed *that* rule!

The quarry hadn't been used for years, and all that remained was a deep pit with smooth stone walls that no one could possibly climb. If you fell in and happened to survive the 40-foot drop to the rock bottom, you would never be able to get back out on your own. Plus, there was a pool of water at the bottom. Going near the quarry just didn't make sense. Almost anything else was a better idea and, on that day particularly, seeing how well the new plane flew was definitely a much better idea.

The model flew well, better than Rick had ever seen a toy airplane fly. Each time he set the plane off on another flight, Rick learned to master its controls until, after an hour or so, the plane was flying for some very impressive distances. *I'm controlling an aircraft!* Rick thought, his heart racing with excitement. *This might be good practice for becoming a pilot.*

"Can I try flying your plane, Rick?" John asked over and over again, but Rick ignored his little brother. After all, to the older boy they were not two kids in a field with a model airplane. Rick was a jet pilot flying across the Atlantic Ocean and that made a nine-year-old easy to ignore.

As the afternoon wore on, a stiff breeze picked up. Newspapers, litter and debris blew across the field. For a while, John considered going home. He wasn't having very much fun and could have been playing with one of his own toys in the basement of their house. Just as he was making up his mind, John heard his brother yell. When John looked around, Rick was nowhere to be found.

"Rick, Rick, Rick!" John called, running first in one direction and then in another. *What if he's fallen into the quarry?* the youngster thought as he ran to the lip of the abandoned pit. He found his brother not *in* the quarry but lying at its edge.

"I flew the plane over the pit. A gust of wind must have knocked it down there. I'm going to have to go down and get it," Rick told his brother.

"Don't!" was all the younger boy could say before his brother spoke again.

"There's an old ladder down at the bottom of the pit. I can see it from here. I'll slide down to the bottom, get the plane and climb back up on the ladder," Rick told John.

"That's just stupid, Rick!" his brother howled. "You're crazy. Even if you don't get killed going down the cliff, there's no way you'll be able to climb back out. That ladder isn't tall enough to reach up here to the top. We should go home and get help. Maybe the fire department can get your plane for you."

Rick paused just long enough to give his brother a cold look before slipping himself, feet first, over the edge of the quarry wall. John turned away. He couldn't watch what he knew would happen next. But soon, he heard a voice—his older brother's voice! John opened his eyes and spun around.

"I made it! I made it!" Rick's voice echoed from the depth of the pit. "The plane isn't too badly broken. I think I can fix it. I'm coming back up right now. If you ever tell anyone about this, I'll punch your lights out!"

Too relieved to speak, John just waved at his brother who was so far down in the pit that he looked like a miniature of himself. *Maybe that's why the old ladder lying down there looks too short to reach the top,* John thought. *Maybe it's just that it's so far down. I hope Rick'll be able to climb back up safely.*

With that thought, the younger boy dared to look down at his brother again.

"John," Rick cried, "the ladder's too big. I can't get it propped up. I need you to come down here and help me. You can do it. Just slide on your backside. I did. It's safe. Nothing will happen. Then we can set the ladder up and both of us can climb out. We'll be safe and no one will ever have to know that we've been down here. Hurry up, will you?"

"Ah, Rick, don't make me do this. I'm scared I'll get hurt and I know we'll get in big trouble," John called to his brother.

"Hurry up, will you? I'm freezing. It's cold down here," Rick called back, sounding much more confident than he felt.

John sat at the edge of the quarry. Then, with an enormous lump filling his throat, he pushed himself off the edge. Seconds later, screaming from the pain of landing on the rocky quarry floor and from relief that he was still alive, John realized he had done what his brother had told him to do. He had done what no other kid except Rick had ever done. Well, no one he'd ever heard about, anyway. He'd descended to the bottom of the pit.

Rick didn't give John much time to consider whether he was pleased or ashamed of his amazing accomplishment.

"Grab the end of the ladder with me," the older boy instructed. "Between the two of us, we should be able to set it up against the quarry wall. Be careful though. Don't back up. There's a big pool right behind us."

Pulling with all their might, the two boys raised one end of the rickety wooden ladder just a bit. Next, they dragged that raised end toward the wall of the cliff. Try as they might, though, the two brothers could not get the heavy wooden ladder propped up past the height of their own hips—it was no use in helping them out of the quarry.

By then, the wind that had blown Rick's plane into the quarry had picked up even more. Gusts of grit swirled around the walls of the pit. The temperature was dropping. The boys were getting tired and frustrated and scared from trying to wrestle something that weighed at least four times more than they did put together. Their fingers were numb. In their hearts, both Rick and John knew that it was hopeless. They weren't going to be able to escape from this pit of a prison. Not without a lot of help, anyway.

Not wanting to admit that he'd made a mistake that had endangered both of their lives, Rick tried to keep going. "I'm going to climb in between these rungs and try to push from there," he told his brother.

As he pulled up on a rung of the ladder, it slid back just an inch or so, but enough to send him crashing backwards into the pool of icy water. He was knocked unconscious.

John panicked. Was his brother dead? He waded into the frigid, filthy water. He grabbed Rick's jacket and pulled until the older boy was at least out of the water. Crying and shivering, John realized that they had no hope of helping themselves. They needed to be rescued.

John screamed for help. Over and over again, he yelled at the top of his lungs. But no one came. His cries echoed throughout the quarry but he knew that because of the steep sides and the strong winds, it was unlikely anyone else could hear his voice. With that realization, John's courage began to seep away until it completely deserted him. He slumped down beside his unconscious brother, with his back against the quarry wall.

There, near John's feet, was Rick's birthday present, the model plane, the whole reason they were in this mess. The plane had looked pretty sharp earlier that day, but it sure didn't look like much now, all bent and cracked and broken from its crash landing at the bottom of the marble pit. John picked it up and examined what remained of it. Without much thought, he spun the propeller over and over again. After a while, it grew so cold in the pit that John's fingers were numb. He set the little plane back down by his feet.

As soon as he did, the broken toy began to vibrate. John didn't think anything of it, because the wind was still blowing. He was even sure it was the wind that caused the plane to move forward a bit after he put it down. But, when the toy plane began to taxi along the quarry floor, the boy sat up straighter. *How can this be happening?* John wondered as he watched the model gain speed and lift off the quarry floor! Soon it disappeared beyond the lip of their stone prison.

I'm seeing things, he thought and closed his eyes. *I might as well sleep for a while. I don't even have the plane to play with anymore.*

John had no idea how dangerously cold he was. He fell into a deep, fitful sleep. He dreamed of warm summer days at the beach and cozy winter evenings reading by the fireplace. All the while, both brothers were dangerously close to freezing.

High above them in the chill windy evening, a man named Sullivan was enjoying a brisk walk with his dog. The man's mind was wandering aimlessly—until a speck in the distant sky caught his eye. Curious, Sullivan walked toward the small object flying over the old marble quarry. Soon, he realized he was seeing a model plane flying in tight circles above the quarry walls. He quickened his pace and hurried to investigate this strange situation more closely.

"What on earth?" he said out loud as got to the quarry's edge. He watched the model plane as it continued to circle. Confused and not entirely comfortable, Sullivan was about to turn around and walk back toward his home when the little toy's flight path changed. Over and over again, the model aircraft plane circled, then dipped into the quarry and back out again. Sullivan looked down into the deep pit, but at first all he could see was darkness. At that very moment, though, one of the boys stirred in his perilously deep sleep.

Realizing that someone, or something, was at the bottom of the pit, Sullivan called down, but the only reply was the echo of his own voice. Even so, the man ran to get help. Less than a half hour later, volunteer firefighters arrived with ladders, ropes and powerful lights. Soon, both Rick and John were at the top of

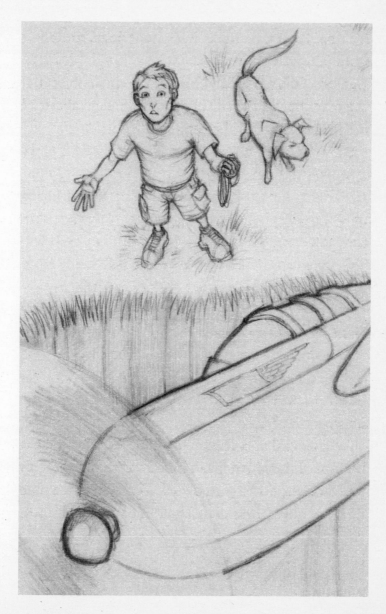

the quarry, wrapped in blankets and being carried to a fire truck.

Impossibly, or so it seemed, the boys' lives had been saved by a toy that acted on its own and attracted the attention necessary to save them.

Although they never talked about it to each other at home, the boys and their parents were all convinced that they knew who had been piloting the little plane that fateful evening. It had been a very special pilot, one they had known and loved and who loved them so much that his spirit had returned to lend a lifesaving hand.

Within a few days, Rick and John had both recovered completely from their misadventure. They never forgot the horrible experience, though, and they never again went near the quarry.

As the years went by, the boys grew up. John became a firefighter and Rick became the pilot that he'd always dreamed of becoming. And every time he settled into a plane's cockpit, he knew with absolute certainty that, just as he had been on that fateful night so many years ago, his grandfather was always flying with him, offering Rick protection from far beyond the skies.

FIDDLER'S PHANTOM

The following ghostly legend from the town of Clinton, New York, has been around for so long that most of the facts—even exactly *which* bridge is the haunted one—have become pretty mixed up.

The tale begins in the early 1800s when a fiddle player was making his way home late at night after playing at a community party. Some people say a murderer lay in wait and that, after killing the fiddler, he hid the musician's lifeless body under a nearby bridge. Another version of the tale reports that the fiddler had indulged in too many spirits of his own at the party. As a result, he lost his balance and fell off the bridge. There, in the water below, he drowned and quickly became a spirit himself.

The bridge soon became known as Fiddler's Bridge. For nearly 100 years, locals made a point to avoid that haunted route after dark for fear of meeting the phantom. Today, however, no one in the area pays much attention to the tale—but that doesn't stop curious and hopeful ghost hunters from driving long distances to see if they can spot the phantom of Fiddler's Bridge.

SUPERNATURAL
AIR SHOW

On a clear night when the moon is full and bright, if you happen to be near Biggin Hill in England's county of Kent, be sure to look up to the heavens. You just might be treated to a spectacular air show from the beyond. On such nights, a squadron of Spitfires, the famous British fighter planes, can sometimes be seen and clearly heard flying across the skies. Perhaps it seems like a perfectly normal sight and sound. After all, airplanes are built to do just that—fly in the sky. These planes, though, are from World War II.

What makes the squadron's appearance even spookier is that often during the day, *after* the eerily mysterious craft have droned about the skies overhead, people who live near Biggin Hill will frequently see strangers in town. These strangers are men in identical trench coats. They will stop local residents on the streets and ask for directions to different spots in town. But just as the people are about to reply, the strangers disappear in a way that no flesh-and-blood person could.

Neither mystery—the World War II Spitfires flying more than 60 years after they were retired, or the well-dressed, vanishing visitors—has ever really been solved. Most folks simply believe that both the planes and the strangers are ghostly echoes from the terrible days of the war. It is believed that the disappearing men in trench coats are the spirits of the pilots who flew the noisy phantom Spitfires above town the night before. Perhaps, for these pilots and their planes, the war has never ended.

SOURCES

The following sources provided direct or indirect inspiration for the stories in this volume.

Alberta Motor Association. *Westworld Alberta,* Volume 29, Number 5, November 2003.

Blackman, W. Haden. *Field Guide to North American Hauntings.* New York: Three Rivers Press, 1998.

Hurrell, Karen, and Janet Bord. *Ghosts.* Glasgow: HarperCollins, 2000.

Look and Learn, December 7, 1963, London.

Martin, MaryJo. *Twilight Dwellers—Ghosts, Ghouls and Goblins of Colorado.* Boulder: Pruett Publishing Company, 2003.

Myers, Arthur. *A Ghosthunters Guide.* Chicago: Contemporary Books, 1992.

Ogden, Tom. *Complete Idiot's Guide to Ghosts and Hauntings.* Indianapolis: Alpha Books, 1999.

Slemen, Tom. *Haunted Liverpool 3.* Liverpool: The Bluecoat Press, 1998.

Smith, Barbara. *Ghost Stories of Hollywood.* Edmonton: Lone Pine Publishing, 2000.

Smith, Barbara. *Ghost Stories of the Sea.* Edmonton: Ghost House Books, 2003.

Taylor, Troy. *Haunted Arizona.* Ghosts of the Prairie, History and Hauntings of America Series. Alton, Illinois: White Chapel Press, 2001.

Tralins, Robert. *Children of the Supernatural.* New York: Lancer Books, 1969.

USA Today, eds. *I Never Believed in Ghosts Until...100 Real-Life Encounters,* Contemporary Books, Chicago, 1992.

ACKNOWLEDGMENTS

My sincere thanks to everyone at Ghost House Books. Thank you for helping my idea become a reality. Please know how much I appreciate your talents and efforts. I'm especially grateful to Grant Kennedy, Shane Kennedy, Nancy Foulds, editors Chris Wangler and Rachelle Delaney, illustrator Aaron Norell and designers Curt Pillipow, Chia-Jung Chang, Gerry Dotto and Elliot Engley.

In addition, special thanks are owed to Bonnie Robbins of Brandon, Manitoba, who sends me story leads that she comes across, and W. Ritchie Benedict of Calgary, Alberta, who just might be the most resourceful paranormal researcher in the world!

Warmest thanks too, go to my family, the core of my life—Bob, Debbie and Robyn—as well as my closet friends, fellow author Jo-Anne Christensen and my skilled but gentle first-line editor Barrie Robinson. Your support makes everything worthwhile.

GHOST HOUSE

Ghost House Books

Add to your ghost house collection with these books full of fascinating mysteries and terrifying tales.

Animal Phantoms: True Ghost Stories *by Barbara Smith*

You'll enjoy these fascinating stories about animal phantoms—some are scary, others are touching, but all are based on real events. In one tale, a fish tank with a mysteriously evil phantom terrifies a boy and his family. In another, a group of foolhardy hikers tease the locals about their superstitions—only to be attacked by a flock of ghostly birds of prey...
$6.95USD/$9.95CDN • 1-894877-52-7 • 5.25" x 7.5" • 144 pages

Horribly Haunted Houses *by Barbara Smith*

Another wonderful bunch of tales of the unexplained by best-selling ghost stories writer Barbara Smith, just for kids! Houses are often considered the most haunted of places and this book makes it clear why. You'll meet young people who live in haunted houses and explore some of the spookiest spaces on the planet...
$6.95USD/$9.95CDN •1-894877-54-3 • 5.25" x 7.5" • 144 pages

Campfire Ghost Stories *by Jo-Anne Christensen*

Great campfire ghost stories, whether read alone or aloud, can raise the hair on the back of your neck. In this scary collection you'll read about glowing orbs of light—the ghostly remains of doomed travelers—that warn a group of campers to leave their campsite or face certain death. In another story, a young girl who grows up with a ghostly double finally discovers the secret behind her extraordinary doppelganger. And there's much more...
$10.95USD/$14.95CDN •1-894877-02-0 • 5.25" x 8.25" • 224 pages

These and many more Ghost House books are available
from your local bookstore or by ordering direct.
U.S. readers call **1-800-518-3541**.
In Canada, call **1-800-661-9017**.